HOORAY FOR
HORRIBLE HARRIET

Leigh HOBBS

BLOOMSBURY

LONDON BERLIN NEW YORK

For Sonya Hartnett,
Horrible Harriet's first champion

Bloomsbury Publishing, London, Berlin and New York

First published in Great Britain in July 2010 by Bloomsbury Publishing Plc
36 Soho Square, London, W1D 3QY

First published by Allen & Unwin Pty Ltd, Sydney, Australia

Hooray for Horrible Harriet copyright © Leigh Hobbs 2005
The moral right of the author/illustrator has been asserted

A CIP catalogue record of this book is available from the British Library

ISBN 978 1 4088 0522 0

10 9 8 7 6 5 4 3 2 1

Printed in China by Toppan Leefung Printing Ltd, Dongguan, Guangdong

Designed by Sandra Nobes and Leigh Hobbs

All papers used by Bloomsbury Publishing are natural, recyclable products
made from wood grown in well-managed forests. The manufacturing processes
conform to the environmental regulations of the country of origin

www.bloomsbury.com/childrens
www.leighhobbs.com.au

It was late, but not everyone was asleep.
Alone in her room, way up in the school roof,
Horrible Harriet was hard at work.
She was adding a secret ingredient to a new dish,
Chicken Surprise.

Suddenly there was a big BOOM!

When the smoke cleared, a strange creature was revealed.
It was Mr Chicken. Horrible Harriet was thrilled.
She had made a friend at last.

Horrible Harriet invited Mr Chicken to stay for dinner.
He gobbled up his octopus pie in one big gulp,
then ate Horrible Harriet's helping, without asking.
Soon there was almost nothing left in the house to eat.

After dinner Mr Chicken sat in Horrible Harriet's favourite spot.
Then he made himself comfortable on her nest.
Horrible Harriet had to sleep standing up.

In the morning, before going downstairs to school,
Horrible Harriet told Mr Chicken to stay inside
and out of sight.
She thought it best to keep her new friend a secret.

In class Horrible Harriet shared her breakfast leftovers,
as Mr Boggle began the day's lesson.

'Good morning, everyone,' he said,
  while Horrible Harriet pretended to be a teapot.

Mr Boggle only ever saw the good side of Horrible Harriet.
He thought she was bold and sweet, smart and friendly.
But everyone else thought Horrible Harriet was…

BIG AND NOISY,
STRANGE AND SCARY!

All too soon it was time for maths.
'Now, class,' said Mr Boggle. 'Three and three is...'
Suddenly there was a tap, tap, tap at the window.

'Oh, who is making that noise?' said Mr Boggle.
'*Some* people aren't paying attention.
Why can't everyone sit still, like Hardworking Harriet?
Now if we add six to three and take away two…'

'… and if we take away seven from ten then add three,
what do we end up with, Helpful Harriet?'
asked busy Mr Boggle.
Just then an extra student joined the class.

'Sounds to me as if *some* people are out of their seats!' said Mr Boggle.

'If I add three to four, and take away two, what do I get?
Class dismissed!' said Mr Boggle as the lunch bell rang.

In the staffroom, the teachers were upset.
Mr Chicken had eaten all their lunches.

Horrible Harriet was upset too.
Mr Chicken had ignored her instructions to stay out of sight.
Not only that, he seemed to be getting bigger by the minute.

Horrible Harriet had gone to a lot of trouble to make
her new friend. But *he* wanted to play with everyone!

Horrible Harriet felt left out.

Mr Chicken had forgotten all about her.
He was busy, showing off and having a good time.

Horrible Harriet knew what had to be done.
It was Mr Chicken's lunchtime and he loved her home cooking.
So she prepared something *extra* special.

Mr Chicken gobbled up Horrible Harriet's special soup
in one big gulp.

Once again there was a BOOM and a big puff of smoke.
But this time it looked like Mr Chicken had disappeared.

Suddenly the teachers and children danced and sang.
Horrible Harriet didn't know what the fuss was about.

There were speeches and flowers and Horrible Harriet
even got a medal. Everyone cheered.
'HOORAY FOR HORRIBLE HARRIET!'
She was the most popular girl at school.

But that didn't last for long.
Soon, once again, everyone thought she was just plain
Horrible Harriet, big and bad, strange and scary.

Of course, Horrible Harriet wasn't overly worried.
She knew that good friends were hard to make ...

...and harder still to keep.
HOORAY FOR HORRIBLE HARRIET!